KT-214-621

STORYTIME COLLECTION

STORYTIME COLLECTION

This book belongs to

_____

_____

Autumn
Publishing

Published in 2018
by Autumn Publishing
Cottage Farm
Sywell
NN6 0BJ
www.igloobooks.com

GUA009 0718
2 4 6 8 10 9 7 5 3
ISBN 978-1-78810-988-8

Printed and manufactured in China

nce upon a time, in a faraway kingdom, a single drop of sunlight fell to Earth and grew into a magical flower. This flower was found by an old woman, who discovered that singing released its magical powers. Being vain and selfish, this woman, called Mother Gothel, kept the flower a secret and, for centuries, used it to restore her youth and beauty.

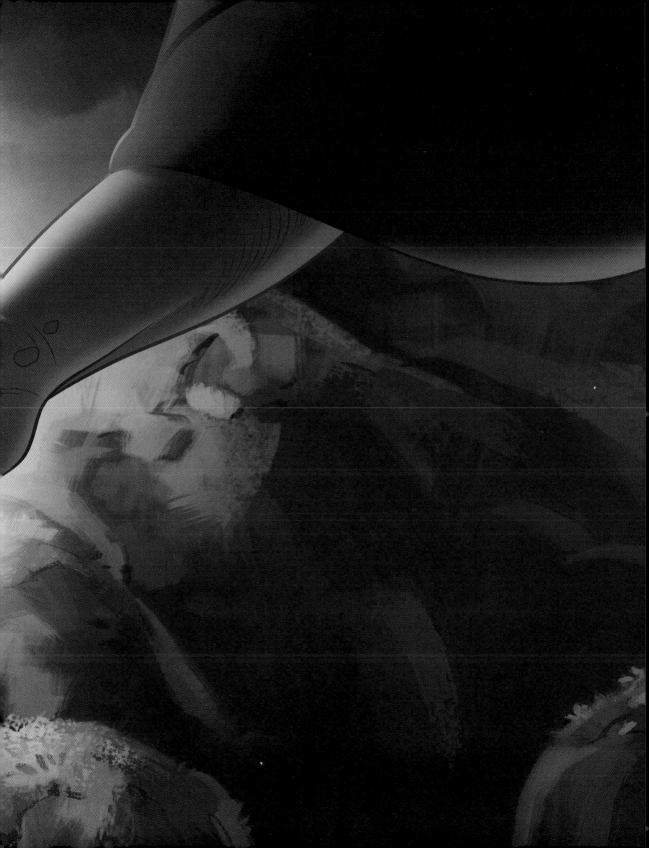

Many hundreds of years after the flower was first discovered, the queen of the kingdom was about to have a baby. However, she fell gravely ill and the townspeople were sent to look for the magical flower that was rumoured to be somewhere in the kingdom.

With so many people looking for it, the flower was quickly found and, much to Mother Gothel's horror, the plant was uprooted and taken back to the castle.

A potion was quickly created and given to the queen, who instantly recovered and gave birth to a beautiful baby girl, who they called Rapunzel. The baby's proud parents then launched a lantern into the sky to celebrate the princess's birth.

That night, desperate to recover
her youth, Mother Gothel crept into the nursery.
Upon finding out the magic was in Rapunzel's hair,
she snipped some off, but it turned brown and lost its magic.
It was then the evil woman decided to kidnap the princess and
take her far away.

The king and queen were heartbroken and, each year, on
Rapunzel's birthday, they released lanterns into the sky, hoping
their lost daughter would see them and return home.

Mother Gothel took Rapunzel to a high tower hidden in a valley and brought her up to believe she was her real mother. "The outside world is a dangerous place," she'd often say, and convinced the princess to remain in the tower in order to protect her hair.

Luckily, Rapunzel found lots of things to do, such as knitting, jigsaws, playing guitar and painting. Though as she approached her eighteenth birthday, she longed for a life outside the tower.

One day, Rapunzel was talking to her 'mother'.
"I want to travel to see the floating lights," she said.
"They appear every year on my birthday. I have to
know what they are."

Mother Gothel lied and said they were simply stars
and nothing very special. She then left the tower-top
home to go and fetch some food for that night's dinner.

Meanwhile, in another part of the forest, a thief named Flynn Rider was on the run with his partners in crime, the Stabbington brothers. They had stolen a crown from the king and queen and their faces were on WANTED posters throughout the land.

Suddenly, the palace guards found them. Flynn decided to ditch the two brothers, but made sure he took the bag containing the crown with him.

Though Flynn escaped the guards, he couldn't escape
Maximus, one of the palace horses. Maximus chased
Flynn to a tree that hung over the edge of a cliff.

CRACK! The trunk, unable to take their weight,
broke away from the ground and the pair of them
fell into the valley.

Both of them survived the fall, but Flynn was able to escape from the persistent horse. Worried Maximus would find him again, Flynn looked for a place to hide and soon came across an enormous tower.

He quickly climbed to the top and jumped inside through an open window. "Alone at last," he said, relieved. Suddenly, everything went black. Rapunzel had hit Flynn on the head with her frying pan!

Flynn was out cold. Though she was scared, Rapunzel felt excited, too! Surely Mother Gothel would let her explore the outside world now she could prove she was able to look after herself.

Wanting to surprise her 'mother' with this news, Rapunzel dragged Flynn across the floor and hid him inside a cupboard.

Rapunzel then noticed something shining inside Flynn's bag. She looked inside and saw the crown. She slowly took it out and placed it on her head. As she looked in the mirror, something about the crown seemed very familiar.

Just then, her 'mother' shouted, "Rapunzel! Let down your hair!" Rapunzel swiftly hid the crown, before letting her mother climb up.

Once her mother was inside, Rapunzel said,
"There's something I want to tell you."

"I hope you're not still talking about the
stars," replied Mother Gothel.

"I'm leading up to that," said Rapunzel,
inching towards the cupboard.

"Enough with the lights, Rapunzel!" shouted Mother
Gothel. "You are not leaving this tower! Ever!"

Rapunzel was shocked. She now knew she had to send her 'mother'
away if she was ever going to see the lights. So, she asked for some paint
as a birthday present, knowing it could only be found far away. Mother
Gothel happily agreed. "I'll be back in three days' time," she said.

With Mother Gothel gone, Rapunzel put
her plan into action. She let Flynn out of the
wardrobe and tied him up using her hair. When he
woke up, Rapunzel told Flynn she'd let him go, only if
he helped her. Pointing to her painting of the floating lights,
Rapunzel said, "Tomorrow they will light the night sky.
You will act as my guide, take me to see them, and return
me home safely. Then, I will return your satchel to you."

Flynn had no choice but to agree.

So, Rapunzel lowered Flynn down with her hair and then climbed down herself. Though she hesitated at first, Rapunzel was so excited to finally be outside the tower for the first time since she could remember. However, she was also full of sadness for betraying her 'mother'.

"Let's just turn around," suggested Flynn, hoping he could get the bag back without having to do anything.

"No!" replied Rapunzel, firmly. "I am seeing those lanterns."

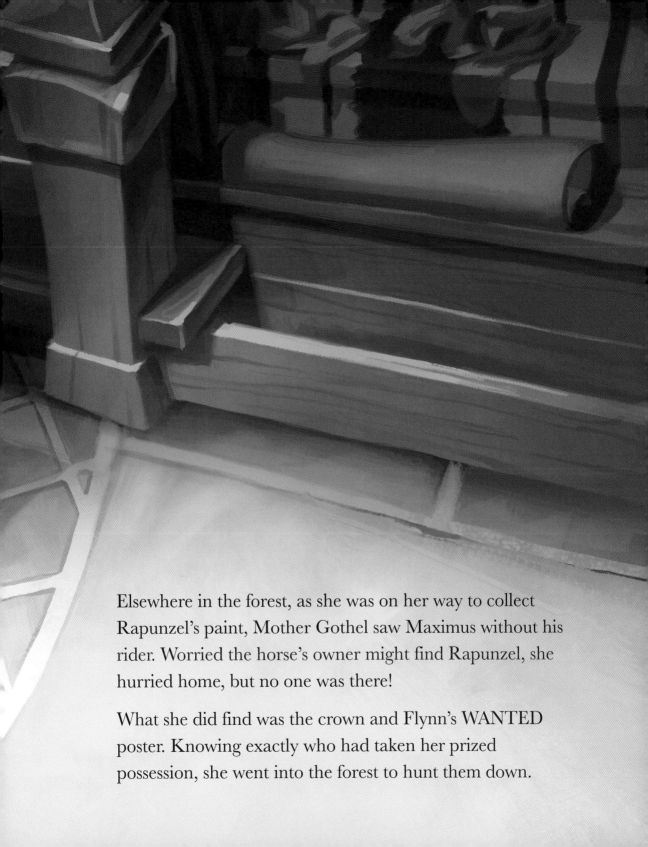

Elsewhere in the forest, as she was on her way to collect Rapunzel's paint, Mother Gothel saw Maximus without his rider. Worried the horse's owner might find Rapunzel, she hurried home, but no one was there!

What she did find was the crown and Flynn's WANTED poster. Knowing exactly who had taken her prized possession, she went into the forest to hunt them down.

As Mother Gothel searched for Rapunzel, she bumped into the Stabbingtons and offered them a deal. "It comes with revenge on Flynn Rider," she added. The two brothers grinned menacingly and readily agreed to help Mother Gothel with her evil scheme.

In a different part of
the forest, Rapunzel was
wrapping her hair around Flynn's hand,
which he'd just cut on a rock. "Don't freak out," she said,
before singing sweetly to her hair. It started to glow and,
within moments, Flynn's hand was healed.

"How long has your hair been doing that?"
asked Flynn.

Rapunzel told him all about her
magical hair and her life up to now.

"You never left that tower," said
Flynn, who was starting to
understand why this trip
was so important
to Rapunzel.

As Flynn searched for firewood, a voice spoke to Rapunzel
from the shadows. "I thought he'd never leave." It was
Mother Gothel. "We're going home, now."

But Rapunzel refused to go. She confessed to liking Flynn and that
she thought he liked her, too. "Why would he like you?" asked Mother
Gothel, laughing. "This is why he's here," she added, passing the crown
to Rapunzel. "Don't let him deceive you."

Mother Gothel dared Rapunzel to give Flynn the crown, telling
her he would leave as soon as he had it back. Then, she headed back
into the dark depths of the forest.

When Flynn returned, Rapunzel said nothing of her
conversation with Mother Gothel.

The next morning, Flynn was rudely awakened. Maximus had found him and grabbed the thief by the foot.

"Let go!" shouted Flynn. Just then, Rapunzel appeared. She begged Maximus to stop chasing Flynn as today was her birthday and he was taking her to see the lanterns. The horse reluctantly agreed.

"You're such a big sweetheart," Rapunzel said to Maximus.

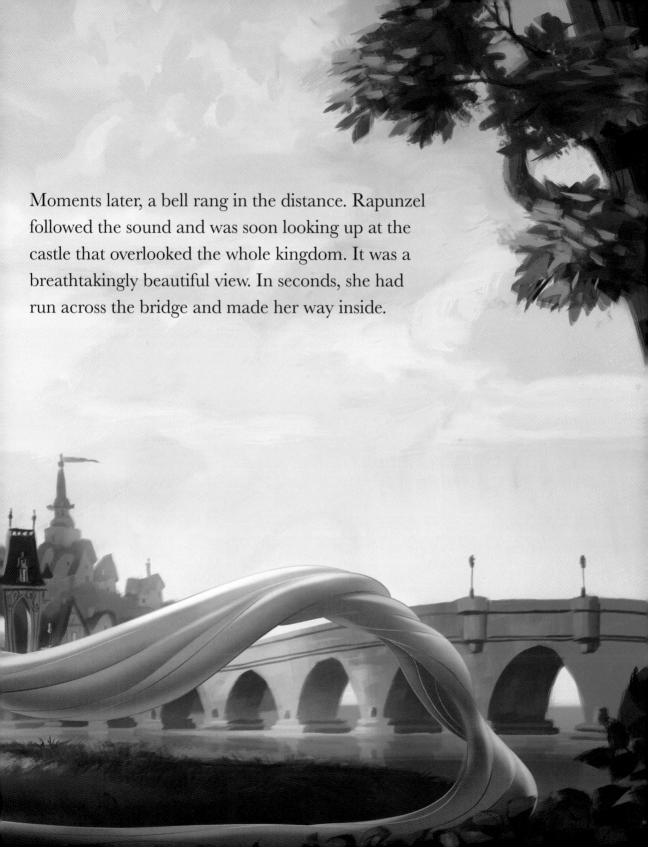

Moments later, a bell rang in the distance. Rapunzel followed the sound and was soon looking up at the castle that overlooked the whole kingdom. It was a breathtakingly beautiful view. In seconds, she had run across the bridge and made her way inside.

As she explored the kingdom, Rapunzel met some children who offered to plait her hair.

A little while later, she became mesmerised by a mosaic on the wall. It was of the king and queen holding a baby girl. "It's the lost princess," explained a young boy. Rapunzel stared closer at the baby's emerald green eyes. They were just like her own.

A few hours later, Flynn took Rapunzel out on a boat.
From out on the lake, the pair had the best view of the kingdom.

Soon, lanterns began to float out of the castle and up into the air.
Rapunzel's heart soared. The view was as beautiful as she always
hoped it would be.

Turning back to Flynn, the princess passed him the bag. She knew
Mother Gothel was wrong, and that he wouldn't leave her once he
had the crown.

As all the lanterns floated away, Flynn spotted the Stabbington brothers on the shore and, without telling Rapunzel why, quickly rowed them back to land. "There's something I have to take care of," he told Rapunzel. "I'll be right back."

Flynn took the bag with him and, on meeting the brothers, gave them the crown. He was giving up his thieving ways so he could be with Rapunzel. However, the brothers knew about the magic hair and wanted it for themselves. Flynn tried to fight them off, but was knocked unconscious and tied up in a boat that was sent sailing into the harbour.

As Rapunzel waited for Flynn, the brothers appeared from the shadows. They told her Flynn had left on a boat with the crown. Upset and fearing for her life, Rapunzel ran, but before she got very far, she heard the sounds of a scuffle, then a voice. "Rapunzel!" It was Mother Gothel.

Rapunzel ran back and saw the two brothers at Mother Gothel's feet. They'd been knocked out. The princess ran to her 'mother', tears in her eyes. "You were right, Mother," said Rapunzel, as they headed home. "You were right about everything."

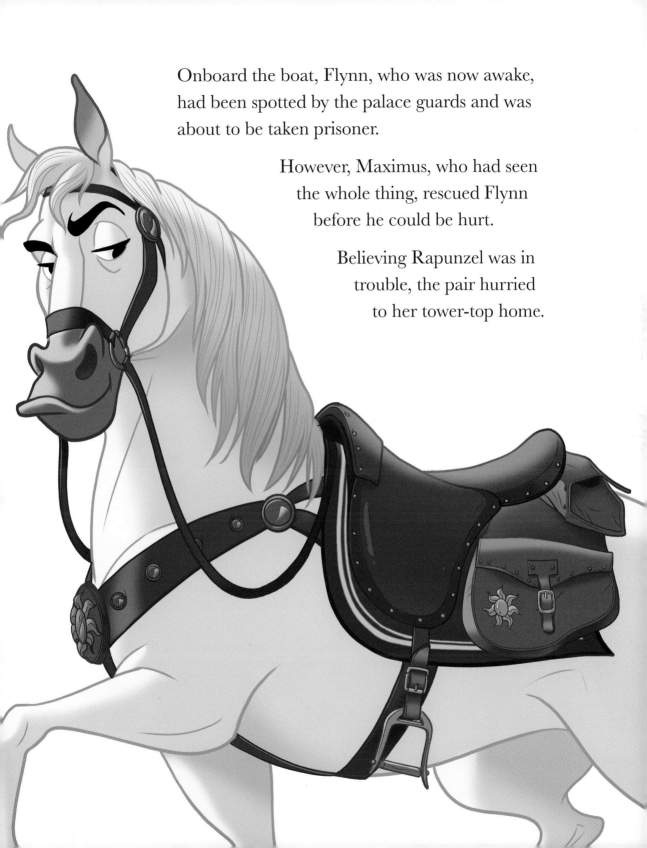

Onboard the boat, Flynn, who was now awake, had been spotted by the palace guards and was about to be taken prisoner.

However, Maximus, who had seen the whole thing, rescued Flynn before he could be hurt.

Believing Rapunzel was in trouble, the pair hurried to her tower-top home.

Now back in the tower, Rapunzel was looking at a flag she'd found on her visit to the castle. On the flag was the symbol of the kingdom. It was then Rapunzel realised she'd been unknowingly painting that same symbol around the walls of her home her entire life!

Suddenly, images flashed through her mind of the lanterns, the mosaic of the lost princess, and finally the crown on her head. It was then Rapunzel realised the shocking truth.

"I'm the lost princess," she said to Mother Gothel, angrily.

"Everything I did was to protect you," said Mother Gothel, desperately trying to justify what she had done.

"I will never let you use my hair again!" cried Rapunzel, pushing her 'mother' into a mirror, sending bits of broken glass everywhere.

However, as Rapunzel tried to leave, Mother Gothel moved threateningly towards her.

Outside, Flynn and Maximus had arrived at the tower. "Rapunzel, let down your hair," called Flynn. There was no reply. He was beginning to wonder if she was even up there when Rapunzel's hair fell from the window. Flynn quickly climbed up. As he hopped inside from the window ledge, he saw Rapunzel was tied up in a chair.

Suddenly, Mother Gothel stabbed Flynn in the back, before placing chains on the wounded man. She then dragged the princess across the floor to a trapdoor that led outside, but Rapunzel resisted.

"For every minute of my life, I will fight. I will never stop trying to get away from you!" she cried. "But, if you let me save him, I will go with you. I promise."

Mother Gothel sneered, but accepted Rapunzel's offer.

Rapunzel rushed to Flynn's side, hoping she wasn't too late to save him. As he gasped in agony, she started to wrap her hair around his wound. "I can't let you do this," said Flynn, who suddenly snatched a piece of broken glass and cut off Rapunzel's hair! It instantly turned brown. With no magic left to sustain her, Mother Gothel started turning to dust, then tripped and tumbled out of the window.

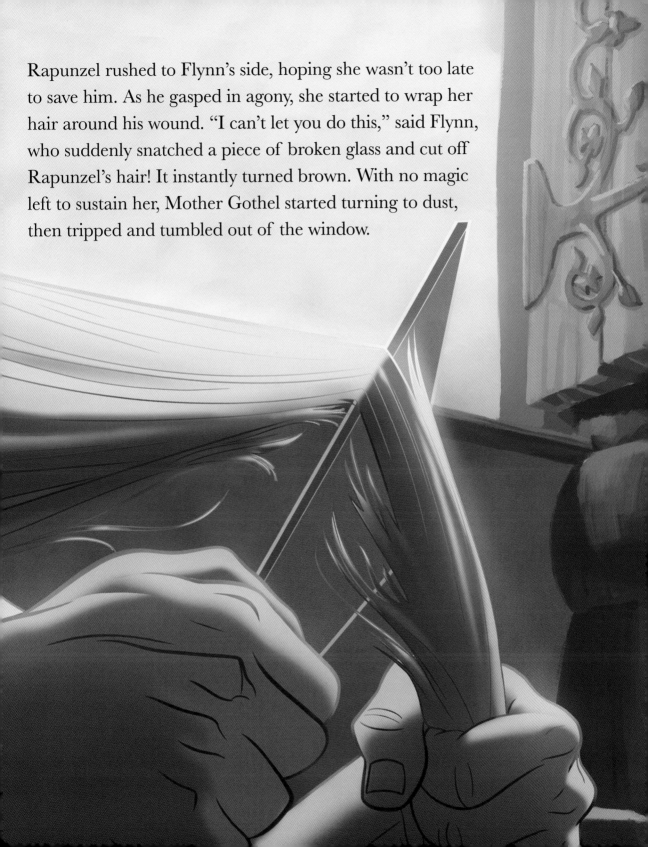

With her hair no longer magical, Rapunzel had no way of saving Flynn's life. As his head dropped back, she knew he was gone. A single tear fell from her face and onto Flynn's cheek. Suddenly, the tear began to glow and golden light covered Flynn's wound, healing him completely.

His eyes opened, slowly. "Rapunzel?" said Flynn.

"Did I ever tell you I've got a thing for brunettes?" He was alive and confident as ever!

The two hugged and shared their first kiss.

Quicker than he'd ever galloped before, Maximus took Rapunzel and Flynn straight to the castle. There, the princess was reunited with her parents after eighteen long years apart. Rapunzel felt her parents' love all around her as they embraced for the first time since she was a baby. They were a family once again.

The entire kingdom rejoiced at the return of the princess and threw a party to celebrate. Hundreds of glowing lanterns were released into the air, their light having finally guided Rapunzel home. Through finding each other, Flynn and Rapunzel had found everlasting love and they both lived happily ever after.

COLLECT THEM ALL!

With 7 more exciting titles to choose from, you'll want to complete your Storytime Collection!

How far will a father go for his son?

Will Simba ever become king?

Will Moana be able to save the ocean?

Can Anna and Elsa stop an eternal winter?

Will Mowgli defeat Shere Khan?

Will the Incredibles save the day?

Will Belle be able to break the curse?